Hi! I'm Michelle Tanner. I'm nine years old. And I just got the best present—a practical joke kit. It's filled with the coolest stuff—garlic candy, disappearing ink, a joy buzzer, and tons more.

With this kit, I'm going to be the best practical joker in the whole world. I'm going to play tricks on everyone in my family. And that's a lot of people.

There's my dad and my two older sisters, D.J. and Stephanie. But that's not all.

My mom died when I was little. So my uncle Jesse moved in to help Dad take care of us. So did Joey Gladstone. He's my dad's friend from college. It's almost like having three dads. But that's still not all!

First Uncle Jesse got married to Becky Donaldson. Then they had twin boys, Nicky and Alex. The twins are four years old now. And they're so cute.

That's nine people. Our dog, Comet, makes ten. Sure it gets kind of crazy sometimes. But I wouldn't change it for anything. It's so much fun living in a full house!

FULL HOUSE™ MICHELLE novels

The Great Pet Project
The Super-Duper Sleepover Party
My Two Best Friends
Lucky, Lucky Day
The Ghost in My Closet
Ballet Surprise
Major League Trouble
My Fourth-Grade Mess
Bunk 3, Teddy and Me
My Best Friend Is a Movie Star! (Super Special)
The Big Turkey Escape
The Substitute Teacher
Calling All Planets
I've Got a Secret
How to Be Cool
The Not-So-Great Outdoors
My Ho-Ho-Horrible Christmas
My Almost Perfect Plan
April Fools!

Activity Book
My Awesome Holiday Friendship Book

Available from MINSTREL Books

FULL HOUSE™
Michelle

April Fools!

Nina Alexander

A Parachute Book

Published by POCKET BOOKS
New York London Toronto Sydney Tokyo Singapore

A MINSTREL PAPERBACK *Original*

A Minstrel Book published by
POCKET BOOKS, a division of Simon & Schuster Inc.
1230 Avenue of the Americas, New York, NY 10020

A PARACHUTE BOOK

READING Copyright © and ™ 1998 by Warner Bros.

FULL HOUSE, characters, names and all related indicia are trademarks of Warner Bros. © 1998.

ISBN: 0-671-01729-2

First Minstrel Books printing April 1998

10 9 8 7 6 5 4 3 2 1

A MINSTREL BOOK and colophon are registered trademarks of Simon & Schuster Inc.

Cover photo by Schultz Photography

Printed in the U.S.A.

April Fools!

Chapter

1

♥ "When is D.J. getting home?" Michelle Tanner cried. "She promised to bring me something from WackyWorld!"

"She should be home any minute," Danny, Michelle's father, answered. He ate the last bite of his chocolate chip cake and carefully set his plate down on the coffee table.

"That's what you said before," Michelle complained. She gave a big sigh that lifted her strawberry-blond bangs off her forehead.

Michelle couldn't wait to see what D.J.

brought her from the amusement park. Her eighteen-year-old sister always gave the best gifts. Michelle was wearing one of D.J.'s presents right then. A T-shirt from D.J.'s college.

"It's such a cool idea to go to Wacky-World on April Fools' Day," Michelle's thirteen-year-old sister, Stephanie, said.

"It is the wackiest day of the year," Aunt Becky agreed. She took a sip of her coffee.

Uncle Jesse began to hum the Wacky-World theme song.

"The dogs go moo, and the cats are blue," Jesse sang.

"At WackyWorld," Danny's friend Joey joined in.

Michelle's uncle Jesse and aunt Becky lived on the third floor of the Tanner house with their four-year-old twin sons, Nicky and Alex. Jesse moved in when Michelle's mom died. Michelle was little then. She couldn't remember a time when Uncle Jesse *hadn't* lived with them.

When he married Aunt Becky, she moved in, too. Michelle loved having Jesse's whole family living in their house.

Joey had also moved in with the Tanners after Michelle's mom died. He was her dad's best friend from college. Michelle loved having him in their house too. He was a comedian, and he kept the whole family laughing.

"Flowers dance, and trees wear pants, at WackyWorld," Joey sang. He jumped up from the sofa. He grabbed Nicky and Alex by their hands and danced around the living room with them.

"Maybe you should leave the singing to me," Jesse told him.

Uncle Jesse used to play in a band. He *does* sing a lot better than Joey, Michelle thought.

Joey began to sing even louder. "The sky is pink—"

"Since you're up, why don't you bring our dessert dishes into the kitchen," Danny interrupted. He winked at Michelle. "Joey's singing won't sound so awful from there."

Michelle giggled. Her dad and Joey loved to tease each other.

"I heard that," Joey sang to Danny. He stacked cake plates and piled empty glasses and coffee cups on top of them.

"Maybe you should make two trips," Danny said. "I don't want you to spill cake crumbs all over my clean carpet." Danny was a nut about keeping the house clean and neat.

Joey sang his answer. "I can handle it. I have an excellent sense of balance."

He stuck Danny's coffee cup on the very top of his pile. Then he slowly walked into the kitchen with his tower of dishes.

"I wonder what D.J. will bring us," Michelle said. "I hope—"

CRASH!

It sounded as though every glass, plate, and bowl the family owned had fallen to the floor and broken.

Comet, the Tanner's golden retriever, gave a high bark.

Danny gasped. "Oh, no!" he cried. "The dishes!"

"Joey? Are you okay?" Michelle shouted. She ran toward the kitchen. The rest of the family ran right behind her.

Michelle skidded to a stop in the kitchen doorway. She looked around, confused. She didn't see even one broken plate. "What happened?"

"Gotcha!" Joey grinned at them. "April Fools."

He held up a portable tape recorder and pushed the play button. A crashing sound filled the kitchen.

Danny groaned. "April Fools' Day. Joey's favorite holiday."

"I forgot all about that silly sound effects tape," Aunt Becky added.

"I remember when Joey got that tape at WackyWorld," Michelle said.

Stephanie shook her head. "I can't be-

5

lieve we fell for it again. Joey used it a million times right after he got it."

"What can I say?" Joey boasted. "I am a master practical joker. I can fool—"

"I'm home," a familiar voice called before Joey could finish.

"D.J.!" Michelle exclaimed. She ran back into the living room. "How was Wacky-World?"

"It was great." D.J. set a large shopping bag on the coffee table. "Gather around. I have something for everyone in here," she announced.

"I hope you didn't bring Joey anything," Danny grumbled. "He doesn't need to get any wackier."

D.J. grinned. "As a matter of fact . . ." She pulled a video out of the bag and handed it to Joey.

Joey read the cover of the video. "Fool your friends with phony news programs and goofy game shows. Cool! I can't wait to try it out. Thanks a lot, D.J."

D.J. reached into the bag again. She handed Danny a WackyWorld apron with flying hamburgers on it.

Stephanie got a neon green oversize T-shirt that said "Kiss me, I'm Wacky" on the front.

D.J. gave Uncle Jesse and Aunt Becky matching WackyWorld sunglasses with fake eyeballs hanging off them.

The twins gave squeals of happiness when D.J. handed each of them a Wacky Walrus stuffed animal.

It must be my turn now, Michelle thought when D.J. reached into the bag again.

Instead of handing Michelle a gift, D.J. pulled out a large bandanna with dancing dogs on it and tied it around Comet's neck.

"What about me?" Michelle blurted out.

"Oh, no. I'm sorry. I forgot all about you!" D.J. wailed.

Michelle stared at D.J. How could her sister have forgotten her? Michelle had

7

been waiting all day to get her special WackyWorld present.

"April Fools!" D.J. cried. "Don't worry, Michelle. I got you the best gift of all—the super-deluxe, extra-special, official Wacky-World practical joke kit."

Michelle felt a big smile spread across her face.

Joey gasped. "No way. I've always wanted one of those."

"Too bad," D.J. teased. "It's Michelle's."

"Awesome!" Michelle cried. "Thanks, D.J."

"You're welcome," D.J. said. "That kit has everything you need to be the greatest practical joker ever. You might even top Joey."

"Yeah, you'd better watch out, Joey," Michelle warned him. "I'm going to be the wackiest joker in this house now."

She shook her head. "No. Wait. Make that the wackiest joker in the whole wacky world!"

Chapter

2

♥ "Please pass me a piece of candy, Michelle," Uncle Jesse said.

"Sure," Michelle answered. She picked the candy dish off the coffee table and handed it to him.

Michelle clamped her teeth together so she wouldn't start giggling. She knew something about those candies that Uncle Jesse didn't know. They came from her Wacky-World joke kit—and they tasted like garlic!

"We just had dessert a couple of hours ago," Aunt Becky reminded Uncle Jesse.

"I know. But I had only one helping,"

9

Uncle Jesse reminded her. He took one of the candies.

Yes! Michelle thought. My first practical joke is about to begin.

"One *large* helping," Danny said.

"Very large," Stephanie added. She turned a page in her history book.

Uncle Jesse dropped the candy back in the bowl.

Michelle slumped down in her chair. Why did everyone have to remind Uncle Jesse about the big dessert he ate? Now her joke was ruined!

Aunt Becky picked up a piece of candy, unwrapped it, and popped it in her mouth.

"Hey!" Uncle Jesse protested. "How come it's okay for *you* to have one?"

Aunt Becky grinned at him. "Because I—" she began.

Then her eyes opened wide.

Yes, yes, yes! Michelle thought.

"This candy . . . tastes like garlic!" Aunt Becky exclaimed.

All right! Michelle felt like cheering.

Aunt Becky grabbed another piece of candy from the bowl and studied it. "What are these things?" she cried. "I love them. We have to get some more."

Huh? Michelle frowned. Garlic candy wasn't supposed to taste good.

"Garlic is one of my favorite seasonings," Danny said. "I add it to almost every recipe." He reached over and took one of the candies. He unwrapped it and stuck it in his mouth.

Michelle stared at him.

Danny closed his eyes as he sucked on the candy. "Mmmm. Garlic candy. What a great idea."

Michelle shook her head. Lucky for me there are lots of other jokes in my kit, she thought. This one was a big flop.

"Time for bed, Michelle," Danny told her.

"Okay," she answered. "Good night, everyone." She stood up and headed for the stairs.

"Good night," everyone called after her.

Michelle hurried up to her room. She pulled her practical joke kit out from under her bed.

She opened the lid and stared at all the practical joke props inside. Which one should she try next?

The trick pen, she decided. It looks like a fun one.

Michelle carefully filled the pen with the special disappearing ink that came with the kit. Then she gently placed the pen on Stephanie's desk.

When Stephanie picked up the pen, it would squirt purple ink all over her. But in a few minutes, the ink would completely disappear. Cool!

Tomorrow I'll figure out tricks to play on everyone else, Michelle thought. It's going to be so much fun!

*   *   *

Michelle bounded down the stairs the next morning. She couldn't wait to start playing her practical jokes.

She hurried into the kitchen and sat at the table. She hung her backpack on her chair. It had a few joke props inside. A good practical joker is always prepared. That's what the WackyWorld booklet in her kit said.

"Michelle, you're just in time for my oatmeal pancakes," Danny told her. He set a plate piled high with pancakes in front of her just as Joey burst through the kitchen door. His face was bright red. He was panting.

"What happened to you?" Danny asked.

Joey took a deep breath. "I took Comet for a walk." Then he shook his head. "Make that—Comet took *me* for a walk."

This is the perfect time to use my dribble glass, Michelle thought. It had dozens of tiny holes in it. The glass would leak all over anyone who drank from it.

Michelle slipped the dribble glass out of her backpack. She ran over to the sink and filled the glass with water.

"Here." She handed the glass to Joey.

Joey took a big gulp of the water. Then another one. He didn't stop drinking until the glass was empty.

He drank the water so fast the glass didn't have a chance to start leaking! Michelle realized.

She sat back down at the table and sighed. My second joke flopped too. I can't believe it, she thought.

"Oh, nooo!" Michelle heard Stephanie shriek.

Then she heard footsteps pounding down the stairs.

The kitchen door flew open and Stephanie rushed in. "Dad!" she wailed. "I just squirted ink all over my white sweater."

"That's horrible!" Michelle cried. She tried not to smile. If she smiled, she might ruin her joke.

I can't wait to see their faces when the ink disappears, Michelle thought. They are going to be totally amazed.

Danny jerked open the cabinet under the sink. He pulled out a bottle of stain remover and tossed it to Stephanie. "Try this," he said. "It's supposed to take out anything."

Stephanie grabbed some paper towels off the counter and soaked them with the stain remover. She wiped at the ink spot.

"Hey, I think it's working," Joey said.

"You're right!" Stephanie exclaimed. "The spot is going away. I don't believe it."

I believe it, Michelle thought. Any stain remover can get rid of *disappearing* ink! I can't believe I've tried three great jokes— and none of them has worked! No one even noticed I was playing a trick.

This is no fun at all.

"Better hurry up and eat, Michelle," Danny said. "You don't want to be late for school."

15

School. That would be a great place to try out her joke kit, Michelle thought. There were tons of people she could play practical jokes on.

Michelle shoveled a big bite of pancake into her mouth. She chewed as fast as she could.

Danny laughed. "Michelle, slow down. You don't have to set a record for speed eating."

"Why not?" Joey said. "In a couple years she could go to the Olympics and we could all watch her on TV."

Stephanie snorted.

Michelle slowed down a little. Not too much, though. She wanted to get to school early.

She had a lot of tricks to play!

Chapter

3

♥ "D.J. gave me an awesome practical joke kit from WackyWorld," Michelle told Cassie and Mandy. They stood near the big double doors leading into their school.

Cassie Wilkins and Mandy Metz were Michelle's two best friends. She had to tell them about her joke kit. She told Cassie and Mandy *everything*.

"What a great present!" Cassie exclaimed. Her brown eyes sparkled.

"What's a great present?" another voice asked.

Michelle spun around and saw Lee

Wagner standing behind her. He was in Mrs. Yoshida's fourth grade class with the girls.

"Michelle's sister gave her a joke kit," Mandy told him. She shoved her curly brown hair behind her ears.

"But don't tell anyone else, okay?" Michelle asked. "If too many people know, it will be hard to play any good tricks."

"What kind of jokes have you played so far?" Lee asked.

Michelle felt her face get hot. She didn't want to tell Lee that none of her jokes had worked.

"I got Stephanie with this special pen that squirts disappearing ink," Michelle said. "She screamed *sooo* loud. She was upstairs, and I heard her all the way down in the kitchen."

Michelle didn't mention the stain remover.

"Awesome!" Lee exclaimed. "What else did you do?"

"I put a bowl of garlic candy on the coffee table," Michelle answered. "My dad and my aunt Becky ate some. You should have seen them. My dad spit the candy all the way across the room. Aunt Becky had to drink three glasses of water!"

Cassie giggled. "Did they get mad?"

Michelle shook her head. "Uh-uh. Not at all."

Wendy Whipple hurried past. "Hi, Wendy," Michelle called.

Wendy gave a tiny smile. "Hi," she mumbled. She pulled her red-and-blue backpack higher on her shoulders and pushed her way through the double doors.

"She doesn't talk much, does she?" Michelle asked.

"And she eats lunch by herself in the hall," Cassie added. "No one else does that."

"It's hard when you're the new kid in school," Mandy said. "You feel like an outsider. I remember."

Mandy transferred to Michelle's school

last year, when they were in the third grade. Wendy had just started at the school last month.

Lee grabbed Michelle by the elbow. "Here comes Jeff. You've got to get him with one of your tricks."

Jeff Farrington was always goofing around, making people laugh. He reminded Michelle of Joey. I bet Jeff will love my jokes, she thought.

Michelle unzipped her blue-and-pink backpack. "I've got the perfect thing," she said. She pulled out a can of peanuts.

"What's funny about peanuts?" Cassie asked.

"There aren't really peanuts in the can," Michelle whispered. "It's full of fake snakes."

"Hey, Jeff," Michelle called. "You want a peanut before class starts? My dad says they are good for your brain."

"Sure," Jeff answered. "I could use extra

help on that math quiz we're having today."
He took the can from Michelle.

Mandy gave a loud cough. She's trying
not to laugh, Michelle realized.

Jeff started to open the can.

Finally, Michelle thought. Here it comes.
A joke that is going to work!

Jeff jerked off the lid. Before Michelle
knew what was happening, he pointed the
can at her.

Three green snakes sprang out at Michelle. She gave a little yelp and jumped
away.

Cassie, Mandy, and Lee cracked up. Lee
laughed so hard he started to choke.

"Great," Michelle mumbled. "I've played
four jokes and not one of them has worked.
Except that last one—but it scared *me*. This
is a disaster!"

"You can't fool me with any of this
stuff," Jeff told Michelle. "I go to the joke
store in the mall all the time. I've seen
every trick they have."

Lee picked up one of the fake snakes and handed it to Michelle. "These things are cool," he said.

Mandy nodded. "They're just springs covered with cloth, but they really looked like snakes when they came flying at you."

Michelle gathered up the other two snakes. She squeezed all three back in the can, then stuck the can into her backpack.

Maybe I can try one more trick before class, she thought.

Then the bell rang.

I guess not. But at lunch, everybody better watch out. Because joke number five is going to work. I know exactly what I'm going to do. This one will be a winner!

Michelle pulled a clay bowl out of her backpack. She set it down in the middle of the cafeteria table.

"What's that?" Jeff said.

Michelle hid a smile. She bet Jeff had never heard of the trick she was about to do. It didn't take any special props. So it wasn't anything Jeff could have seen in the joke shop.

"It's a bowl from Hawaii," she told him. "It's very old."

Well, at least a few months old, Michelle thought. D.J. made the bowl in a pottery class she took at college.

"There's a secret about this bowl," Michelle continued.

"A secret?" Mandy asked.

Michelle nodded. "I'll show you. But first I have to fill it with water."

Michelle picked up the bowl and walked over to the water fountain. She filled the bowl almost to the top. Then she went back and set the bowl down in the center of the table.

"Are you ready to hear the secret?" Michelle asked.

Cassie nodded. Her brown eyes were open wide.

"Hurry up and tell!" Mandy cried.

Anna Abdul, Erin Davis, and Mary Beth Alonzo crowded behind Cassie and Mandy. "Can we hear too?" Anna asked.

Michelle pretended to think about it. "I guess it would be okay," she finally answered.

Michelle placed her hands on the bowl. "Some people believe there are spirits that live in water," she told the other kids. "I believe it too. Because I've heard the spirits talking."

"No way," Lee said.

"It's true," Michelle said. "There is something special about this bowl. When you put water in it, it lets you hear the spirits in the water."

Michelle bent over the bowl. She closed her eyes and pretended to listen hard. "I can hear their voices already."

"Really?" Jeff asked. "You can hear them right now?"

Michelle opened her eyes a crack and peeked at Jeff.

24

He leaned toward the bowl.

Not quite close enough. Michelle needed him to move his face a little nearer—so she could splash him!

"Their voices are very tiny. You have to be really close to hear them," Michelle said. She moved back to give him room.

Jeff leaned closer. His head almost touched Michelle's.

I've got you now, Michelle thought.

Splash!

Chapter
4

♥ Jeff smacked his hand down on the water in the bowl. Drops sprayed all over Michelle's face.

"Hey! You splashed me!" Michelle cried.

"Are you sure the water spirits didn't do it?" Jeff teased.

Michelle stared around the table. Cassie, Mandy, Lee, Anna, and Mary Beth were all laughing at her.

Cassie handed Michelle one of her napkins. Michelle wiped off her face.

I guess it *did* look pretty funny, she thought.

"You got me good," Michelle admitted to Jeff.

Jeff grinned at her. "I told you I know every joke. The guy who works at the joke store told me about that spirit-in-the-water trick last year."

Michelle pushed her wet bangs off her forehead.

I was right, she thought. Trick number five *did* work. But not the way I thought it would. The joke was on me—again!

"None of my jokes worked the way they're supposed to work. Maybe I should just give up!" Michelle muttered as she trudged through the front door of her house. She walked into the living room, flopped down on the couch, and gave a big sigh.

Joey glanced up from the magazine he was reading. "You look like you need a joke," he told Michelle.

She groaned. She didn't even want to hear the word *joke* right now.

"What goes ha, ha, ha—plop?" Joey asked.

"I don't know," Michelle muttered.

"A man laughing his head off," Joey answered.

Michelle tried to smile. She knew Joey was trying to cheer her up—but she didn't feel much like laughing.

"Is something wrong?" Joey asked. "I know my joke was funnier than that!"

"D.J. gave me that cool practical joke kit, but I haven't been able to play one good joke!" Michelle burst out. "Something always goes wrong."

"What you need are a few lessons from Professor Joey. I know everything there is to know about playing jokes," Joey bragged.

Michelle sat up. "That would be great," she said.

Joey stood and began to pace in front of the couch as he talked. "The most important thing is surprise. So when you choose your next victim, make it someone who has never seen you play a practical joke."

"But everyone in the family has seen *you* play jokes, and you still play jokes on us," Michelle protested.

"You're just a beginner," Joey said. He grinned at her. "I'm a master."

Michelle nodded. She pulled her binder out of her backpack. She flipped it open and began taking notes.

"It would be better if it's someone who doesn't even know you have a practical joke kit," Joey continued.

Michelle wrote as fast as she could.

"Don't do a joke where you have to talk a lot," Joey said. "And when you *do* talk, make sure to look the other person in the eye."

Michelle began to smile. With Joey's advice, she was going to be able to play a great joke on one of the kids at school.

Joke number six was going to be perfect.

Chapter
5

♥ Michelle couldn't sleep that night. She lay awake, staring at the ceiling and wondering who she should play a joke on next. Anna Abdul? Mary Beth Alonzo?

No. They'd seen her try the magic bowl trick. They would be looking out for another joke.

She remembered what Joey said. It had to be someone who didn't know she even owned a practical joke kit.

Michelle sat up suddenly. She knew the perfect person.

Wendy Whipple!

Wendy didn't see the trick yesterday. And she didn't know about the kit.

Playing trick six on Wendy will make her feel like part of the group, Michelle thought. After the trick, she won't feel like such an outsider anymore.

Yes. Definitely—Wendy.

The next day at lunch Michelle stopped Mandy and Cassie in the hall outside their classroom.

"There's Wendy. I'm going to try the disappearing-ink joke on her," Michelle whispered. She pulled the trick pen out of her pack.

Wendy was sitting beside the classroom door, eating a sandwich. Michelle hurried over to her. Cassie and Mandy followed.

"Hey, Wendy," Michelle said. She looked Wendy in the eye. "Want to see the pen my big sister gave me?"

Wendy looked surprised. "Sure," she said. She scrambled to her feet.

Michelle held the pen out to Wendy. Then she pushed a little button on one side.

Bright purple ink squirted out. It splattered across Wendy's yellow dress. Wendy's eyes opened wide with surprise.

Yes, I did it! Michelle thought. She felt like jumping up and down. Finally one of my practical jokes worked.

Then Wendy let out a scream. "My dress!"

"It's okay. It's not real," Michelle started to explain. "It's just a joke."

"My dress! My dress!" Wendy kept screaming.

Mrs. Yoshida burst out of the classroom. "What happened?" she demanded.

"Michelle squirted ink all over me!" Wendy cried.

"But I told you—it was just a joke," Michelle repeated. "It was funny."

Wendy's eyes filled with tears. "No, it wasn't. It wasn't funny at all," she wailed. "Michelle, you're the meanest person I ever met!"

Chapter 6

♥ "Tell me what happened, girls," Mrs. Yoshida said.

By now Jeff, Lee, and a couple other kids had wandered over. They stared at Wendy and Michelle. "What's going on?" someone murmured.

"Michelle ruined my dress. It's new. My mom just got it for me." Wendy sniffled. A tear ran down her cheek.

Oh, no! What have I done? Michelle thought. She felt her stomach twist into a million knots. I didn't mean to make Wendy cry. I meant to make her laugh. This is terrible!

"I—I—" Michelle wanted to explain what had happened. But the words wouldn't come out.

"Michelle didn't mean to make Wendy cry," Mandy said.

"I know that. I'm sure it was an accident," Mrs. Yoshida said. She took Wendy by the arm. "Why don't we go in the bathroom and try to clean you up."

Wendy jerked away. "It wasn't an accident!" she yelled. "Michelle did it on purpose."

Michelle swallowed hard. She had to make Mrs. Yoshida understand.

"I did squirt Wendy on purpose," Michelle admitted. "But it was a joke. I used disappearing ink. It will fade away in a few seconds."

"Yeah," Cassie added. "Don't worry, Wendy. Your dress is going to be fine."

"We thought you would think it was funny," Mandy added.

"Look, Wendy," Mrs. Yoshida said. "The ink is already much lighter."

Wendy gave another big sniffle.

The bell rang.

"Why don't you run to the bathroom and wash your face before class starts," Mrs. Yoshida told Wendy. "You'll feel better."

"I'm sorry, Wendy. I didn't mean to upset you," Michelle said.

Wendy didn't answer. She spun around and ran down the hall toward the bathroom.

Michelle stared up at her teacher. "I'm really sorry."

"I know you are," Mrs. Yoshida answered. "It can be fun to play jokes. But you have to think about how the other person is going to feel."

Michelle stared up at her teacher. "I'm really sorry," she whispered again. It was all she could think of to say.

"School is not the right place for practical

jokes, anyway. I'll keep the pen with the disappearing ink until the day is over," Mrs. Yoshida said.

She held out her hand and Michelle gave the pen to her.

"Good thing she doesn't know about the other stuff," Jeff whispered to Lee as they headed into the classroom.

Mrs. Yoshida turned toward him. "What did you say, Jeff?

"Um, nothing." Jeff stared down at the floor.

"Jeff, answer my question please," Mrs. Yoshida said firmly.

"Um, it's just that Michelle has some other joke stuff besides the disappearing ink," Jeff mumbled.

"Is that true, Michelle?" the teacher asked.

Michelle unzipped her backpack. She pulled out the can of fake snakes and a whoopie cushion and gave them to Mrs.

Yoshida. "I have a couple other things in my desk," she admitted.

"I'll need to hold all of them for you until class is over," Mrs. Yoshida said. She led the way into the classroom.

Michelle shuffled over to her desk and opened the top. She pulled out a joy buzzer and a plastic spider. She hurried up to Mrs. Yoshida and handed them to her.

"School isn't the place for pranks, Michelle," her teacher said. "After today I don't want to see these things again."

"You won't," Michelle said quickly. "I promise."

Michelle headed toward Mrs. Yoshida's classroom the next morning. Her backpack felt light without her joke props inside.

"Hi, Michelle," Jeff called from the drinking fountain. He turned on the water and brought his ear close to the stream. "The water spirits say 'hi' too."

"Very funny," Michelle called back.

Jeff trotted over to her. "I'm sorry about yesterday," he said. "I didn't mean for Mrs. Yoshida to hear me say you had more joke stuff at school."

"That's okay," Michelle answered. "She was really nice when she gave me everything back after school. She told me she knew I didn't mean to hurt Wendy's feelings."

Michelle spotted Cassie, Mandy, and Lee. She and Jeff hurried over to them.

"So what tricks did you play on your family last night?" Lee asked her.

"I decided I'm never playing another practical joke again," Michelle said. "I gave Joey my WackyWorld kit."

"You gave all that cool stuff away?" Jeff exclaimed.

Michelle shrugged. "Playing jokes wasn't as much fun as I thought it would be."

A loud scream echoed through the hallway.

"What was that?" Cassie gasped.

Erin Davis ran toward them. Her face was pale.

"The drinking fountain is full of spiders!" she cried.

Chapter

7

♡ Everyone raced to the drinking fountain.

"Erin's right!" Lee exclaimed. "There are about a million spiders in there."

Michelle peered over his shoulder. Big black spiders clogged the drain of the drinking fountain. "Yuck," she muttered.

"Gross!" Cassie gasped.

Then Michelle leaned closer. There was something weird about those spiders.

"Hey, none of them are moving," she said. "Are you sure they're real?"

Lee poked one of the spiders with a pencil. It didn't even twitch. "They're plastic!" He grabbed a handful of the spiders and tossed them at Michelle. "Think fast!" he cried.

Michelle jumped away. "Very funny," she grumbled.

"Hey, look at this," Mandy called. She held up a crumpled piece of paper. "I found it here on the floor by the fountain."

Michelle took the piece of paper and studied it.

More plastic spiders were glued to the paper. Right in the middle, someone had drawn a grinning mouth with big teeth.

Michelle read the big black letters printed underneath the mouth.

" 'Signed, the Joker.' Who's the Joker?" she asked.

Jeff laughed. "You should know," he answered.

Huh? Then Michelle realized what Jeff meant.

"I didn't do it!" she cried. "It wasn't me."

Lee shook his head. "What a great fake-out. I totally believed you when you said you weren't playing any more tricks."

"But I *didn't* do it!" Michelle insisted.

"Oh, come on, Michelle," Erin called. "Everybody knows you did. You squirted Wendy with that disappearing ink yesterday. And you tried to get us with that water-spirit trick."

"Time to go inside, everyone," Mrs. Yoshida called.

Michelle glanced over her shoulder. Mrs. Yoshida was halfway down the hall.

I can't let her see me with these spiders. Not after what happened yesterday, Michelle thought.

She bent down, scooped up all the spiders, and stuffed them in her backpack. Then she rushed inside.

Michelle shoved her backpack in one of the cubbies in the back of the room. She hurried to her desk and plopped down in her seat.

Mrs. Yoshida began to call roll.

Mandy tossed a tiny ball of paper onto Michelle's desk. Michelle opened it and read the note Mandy had written. "I believe you," it said.

Michelle glanced over at Mandy and smiled. "Thanks," she whispered.

"Okay, take out your math workbooks and turn to page thirty-three," Mrs. Yoshida said. "I'm going to call some of you up to do problems on the board. Evan Burger—problem number one. Michelle Tanner—problem number two. . . ."

Michelle didn't listen to the rest of the names. She grabbed her workbook and headed to the front of the class.

Michelle copied the problem onto the board. She figured out the answer and wrote it down, too. Then she returned to her seat.

"Good job, everyone," Mrs. Yoshida said. "Now, let's go over these one by one."

She reached for a piece of chalk. Then she gave a little gasp and jerked her hand back. "A spider!"

Mrs. Yoshida peered closely at the chalk tray. Then she picked the spider up by one leg and showed it to the class. "A fake one, thank goodness. But what's this?"

She picked up a folded bit of paper that was under the spider. Unfolding it, she read aloud: " 'Signed, the Joker. Get ready for my next trick!' "

The Joker? Who *is* that? Michelle wondered.

A couple of kids snickered.

Erin turned around in her seat and stared at Michelle.

Lee grinned at Michelle. "Good one."

Michelle sank down in her seat. She knew they thought she had put the spider there. But she hadn't!

Mrs. Yoshida dropped the plastic spider

into her top desk drawer. "Would anyone like to tell me how that spider got in the chalk tray? And who left that note?" she asked.

Silence filled the room. Mrs. Yoshida glanced around. Michelle thought her teacher stared at her just a few seconds longer than any of the other kids.

Michelle felt her cheeks turn red. She wanted to stand up and yell that she didn't do it. She kept quiet instead.

"All right," Mrs. Yoshida finally said. "As far as I'm concerned, we'll forget about this—for now. But there had better not be a next time. I don't want any more practical jokes in this classroom. Understood?"

Michelle nodded, along with all the other kids in the class.

Mrs. Yoshida went over the math problems on the board. Then she called up another group of students.

Michelle couldn't pay attention. She couldn't stop thinking about those spiders.

The ones in the drinking fountain—and the one in the chalk tray.

Who put them there? Who was the Joker?

All Michelle knew for sure was that *she* wasn't—and that a lot of people thought she was. Even Mrs. Yoshida.

Then she thought of something else.

In the second note, the Joker said, "Get ready for my next trick." So whoever it was, he or she was planning to play more practical jokes.

If Michelle didn't look out, *she* would be the one who got in trouble.

Michelle stared around the room. The real Joker is in here somewhere, she thought. I know it.

It couldn't be Cassie or Mandy. They would have told me.

Erin screamed really loud when she saw the spiders in the drinking fountain. I don't think she was faking it. So she's not the practical joker.

Lee wouldn't say *I* played that trick if he did it himself. That would be too mean. So he's not the Joker either.

Mary Beth hates spiders, Michelle remembered. I bet she would be afraid to pick one up—even if it was made of plastic. That leaves her out.

Jeff . . .

Hmmm, Michelle thought.

Jeff loves practical jokes.

Michelle sat up a little straighter. He was over by the drinking fountain this morning! she remembered.

That's it, she thought.

Jeff must be the Joker!

Chapter

8

♥ "Should I tell Mrs. Yoshida about Jeff?" Michelle asked Mandy and Cassie that afternoon. "I don't want to get him in trouble. But I don't want to be blamed for his jokes, either."

"We're not positive Jeff *is* the Joker," Cassie said.

"That's true." Michelle frowned. "It wouldn't be right to tell if I wasn't positive." Her eyes brightened as an idea hit her. "I know. We'll get proof."

"How?" Mandy asked.

"We'll secretly follow him," Michelle explained. "If he tries to play a joke tomorrow, we'll see him setting it up. And then we've got him."

The next morning Michelle arrived in school prepared to follow Jeff. She met Mandy and Cassie down the hall from Mrs. Yoshida's class.

"Here's a pair of binoculars for you," she said, handing Cassie a pair of green plastic binoculars. "And one for you." She handed Mandy a red pair.

"Cool," Mandy exclaimed. "Where did you get these?"

"They're prizes from a cereal box," Michelle said. "I had to open two extra boxes to get all three pair. My dad was kind of annoyed at me, but it was worth it." She slung a pair of yellow binoculars around her neck.

"So we're all set," Cassie said. She started walking toward the classroom.

"Wait. Disguises!" Michelle dug into her

backpack. She pulled out baseball caps and sunglasses. She handed one of each to Mandy and Cassie. Then she put on her own hat and sunglasses. "With this stuff on, Jeff won't even know who we are!"

"Here he comes," Mandy warned. Jeff walked toward them.

"Watch. He won't recognize us," Michelle whispered.

Jeff stopped right beside them. "Hi, Michelle. What's with the goofy shades and the cap?"

Michelle lifted her sunglasses from her face. "Oh, I . . . I . . . I thought it might be a cool look."

Jeff shrugged. "I guess so. See you in class."

Oooops! Michelle thought.

As Jeff walked away, the girls took off their caps. They tossed the sunglasses back into Michelle's backpack.

"All right, so the disguises didn't work,"

Michelle admitted. "But we can still follow him."

In class Michelle kept her eyes fixed on Jeff. If he plays any jokes, I'm going to see them, she thought.

Jeff didn't play any jokes. All he did was listen to Mrs. Yoshida and doodle in his notebook. Once he did throw an eraser at Lee when Mrs. Yoshida wasn't looking.

When the bell rang for recess, Jeff hurried out.

Michelle pushed Mandy and Cassie out the door. "After him!"

The girls ran outside to the playground. Jeff was kicking a soccer ball around with a bunch of other kids.

"Cassie, you stay here by the door," Michelle ordered. "Mandy, you guard the gate, just in case he tries to sneak out. Both of you watch him through your binoculars."

"What are you going to do, Michelle?" Mandy asked.

"I'm going to follow him," Michelle explained.

Following Jeff was hard. Especially because Michelle was trying to look like she *wasn't* following him. She strolled around the school yard, whistling and gazing up at the sky.

"Hey, watch where you're going," Darren Bates grumbled when Michelle bumped into him for the second time.

"Yeah, Michelle. You just stepped on my toe. What's your problem?" Keesha Roberts asked.

"Sorry," Michelle murmured. She hurried away.

Now, where did Jeff go? Michelle scanned the playground. She finally spotted him on the other side, near the fence.

She drifted slowly toward him, trying to look casual. "You're in my way!" Alvin Chu snapped as he darted past her.

Michelle frowned. Why was Alvin so rude?

"Michelle!" someone screamed behind her. *"Look out!"*

Michelle glanced over her shoulder.

Uh-oh. A soccer ball was zooming straight toward her!

BONK! It bounced off the top of her head—and then it bounced right over the fence. Out onto the sidewalk.

"Oh, no," Michelle gasped.

One of the school yard monitors hurried out to get the ball. Everyone else crowded around Michelle, yelling at her.

"Smooth move!" Paul Browne said. "You ruined my goal shot. Why were you just standing there in the middle of our game?"

Michelle felt her cheeks turning red. "Sorry," she mumbled. She had been so busy watching Jeff that she hadn't even realized there was a game going on.

Hey! Where *was* Jeff? Michelle quickly glanced around.

She didn't see him anywhere.

She waved to Cassie and Mandy. They met her by the doors.

"Where did Jeff go?" Michelle demanded.

Cassie shrugged. "I didn't see," she said. "There was dirt on my binoculars. I was trying to clean them."

"I was watching you get hit by the ball," Mandy admitted.

Michelle sighed. "Come on," she said. "Let's look for him."

They couldn't find Jeff anywhere inside. Finally Cassie spotted him walking down the hall with Lee. A minute later the bell rang. It was time for class again.

Michelle checked her watch. "We lost Jeff for ten minutes," she said. "That was enough time for him to set up a joke."

"I hope he didn't," Mandy murmured.

"Me, too," Michelle said. "Because you know who Mrs. Yoshida will blame if something happens."

"You," Cassie said.

"Me," Michelle agreed with a sigh.

Chapter

9

💙 All through math class, Michelle worried. Did Jeff set up another joke?

If he did, what was it? Plastic worms in the hot lunch?

"Put your math homework away," Mrs. Yoshida called at last. "It's time to read another chapter in our book."

Michelle started to feel a tiny bit better. Mrs. Yoshida was in the middle of reading them a book about the Underground Railroad. It was really exciting. Michelle couldn't wait to find out what happened next.

Mrs. Yoshida walked over to the bookcase by the windows. She picked up the book.

Then she frowned.

"I'm afraid I won't be able to read to you today," she announced, holding up the book. "Someone glued the pages together."

Mrs. Yoshida held up a sheet of paper that had been placed underneath the book. Michelle could see the big black letters from her seat: SIGNED, THE JOKER.

"This is not a funny joke," Mrs. Yoshida said sternly. "This book is ruined."

"Now we'll never find out how the story ends," Erin complained.

"That was a rotten trick," Lee muttered.

The classroom filled with whispers. All the kids kept glancing over at Michelle.

Oh, no! Everyone thinks *I* did this, Michelle thought. A knot formed in her stomach.

"We'll have quiet reading time instead," Mrs. Yoshida announced. "Take out one of your own books or pick one from the class library."

Michelle reached into her desk and pulled out the mystery book she was reading.

Mrs. Yoshida walked over to her. "Michelle, I'd like to talk to you in the hall," she said quietly.

Chapter
10

❤ Michelle's heart sank. She tiptoed out of the classroom after Mrs. Yoshida. Mrs. Yoshida shut the door behind them.

"I called you out here because I thought maybe you had something to tell me that you didn't want the whole class to hear," Mrs. Yoshida said.

Michelle knew what Mrs. Yoshida wanted to hear. She wanted Michelle to admit that she had played all those tricks.

But she hadn't!

"I didn't glue the book together. I really wanted to hear the end of the story just like everyone else," Michelle cried. "And I didn't put the spider in the chalk tray either. Really, Mrs. Yoshida."

Mrs. Yoshida stared at her for a long moment. Michelle shifted from foot to foot. She didn't know what else to say. She didn't know how to convince Mrs. Yoshida she was telling the truth.

"All right," Mrs. Yoshida finally said. "If you say you didn't play those tricks, I believe you." She hesitated. "But I know playing practical jokes can be a lot of fun. It can be hard to know when to quit."

Michelle didn't say anything.

Mrs. Yoshida sighed. "Let's go back inside."

Michelle crept into the classroom and slid into her seat.

Mrs. Yoshida had been nice to her, but Michelle didn't think her teacher really believed her.

What if there's another joke? Michelle wondered. I could be in big trouble.

This was serious. She had to clear her name. She had to prove Jeff was the one playing the jokes.

She had to do it before the Joker struck again!

At home, Michelle went up to the bedroom she shared with Stephanie. Stephanie was working on a project on her computer.

"What are you doing?" Michelle asked.

"Writing an article," Stephanie replied. She was a reporter for her school paper. "It's called 'Exactly What Is Lunch Meat Surprise?' I had to go undercover to get the story."

"You went undercover?" Michelle gasped, impressed. "You mean, like, you disguised yourself as someone else?"

"Not exactly," Stephanie admitted. "But I did sneak into the lunchroom kitchen on the day they were preparing it. I stood there a whole five minutes before they noticed me."

"What *is* Lunch Meat Surprise?" Michelle asked.

"Ground up leftovers from the day before, plus a ton of bread crumbs. It's gross," Stephanie said, wrinkling her nose.

Michelle frowned. "Steph, you're a reporter. How would you find out something about a person? Something they're trying to keep a secret."

Stephanie tossed her blond hair back over her shoulder. "Hmmmm. I guess I'd follow him."

"I tried that," Michelle said. "It didn't go too well."

Stephanie smiled. "Too bad you can't wear a wire."

"A what?" Michelle asked.

"A wire," Stephanie repeated. "They do it on police and spy shows on TV. The good guys hide a small tape recorder under someone's clothes. Then they send that person in to talk to the suspect. They listen on

62

a radio somewhere else and hope the suspect will admit he or she did the crime."

"Why would the suspect say something dumb like that?" Michelle asked.

"Because the suspect trusts the person he's talking to and doesn't know he's being taped," Stephanie explained.

"Ohhhhh," Michelle breathed. "I get it."

"But you don't have that kind of fancy equipment," Stephanie added. "Too bad."

She turned back to her report. Michelle stretched out on her bed with her hands tucked under her head, thinking hard.

Wearing a wire. That sounded like a good plan.

It was true that she didn't have any fancy equipment.

Maybe there was a way to pull it off anyway.

Chapter

11

♥ "It will be easy," Michelle told Mandy. "Really."

It was lunchtime the next day. Michelle and her friends were in the school lunchroom. Michelle held a pair of walkie-talkies she had borrowed from Lee.

"All you have to do is hide this walkie-talkie under your shirt and talk to Jeff. I'll be listening on the other end," Michelle explained. "As soon as you get him to admit he's the Joker, you can stop. I'll have my proof."

"How is Mandy supposed to get him to admit that?" Cassie asked.

"Talk to him about jokes," Michelle suggested. "Ask him if he's gotten any cool stuff from the joke store lately."

"But why do *I* have to do it?" Mandy groaned.

"Well, I can't do it," Michelle pointed out. "Jeff wouldn't tell *me* if he's the one playing the tricks. He knows I'm being blamed. He'd be afraid I would tell on him."

"Would you tell on him?" Mandy asked.

"No," Michelle said. She had thought hard about that. "I'll just tell him I have proof he's the one behind the jokes, and he has to stop. But if he plays another trick, I will tell."

Mandy frowned. "Well . . ." she said.

"Please?" Michelle begged.

"Oh, okay," Mandy said at last.

"Thanks." Michelle beamed at her friends. "I know this is going to work. Isn't it a great idea?"

She looked at her friends, waiting for them to agree.

They didn't say anything.

"What's the matter?" Michelle asked, her smile fading.

"I don't like this idea of spying on Jeff," Cassie said. "Following him was one thing. But listening secretly . . ."

"It doesn't seem right," Mandy added. "He is our friend, after all."

Michelle rested her chin on her hands. "I know, but what else can I do?"

Mandy and Cassie didn't answer.

"I guess I could wait to see what happens today," Michelle said after a few minutes. "If he doesn't pull another practical joke, then maybe it's all over."

"Good idea," Mandy said. "You might not have to do anything at all."

That would be great, Michelle thought.

She had a bad feeling her problem wasn't going to go away that easily.

After lunch Michelle went to class a few

minutes early. She was thinking so hard she walked right into Anna Abdul's desk. Anna's four sharpened pencils lay on the desk, neatly lined up, as always.

Michelle was nearly at her own desk when she realized something was strange.

Anna's pencils hadn't moved when Michelle bumped into the desk. Not one of them had rolled even an inch.

Michelle went back to Anna's desk. She reached to pick up a pencil.

She couldn't lift it.

She tried another. It wouldn't budge, either.

Anna's pencils were glued to her desk!

Anna sat right up front. Mrs. Yoshida would see her trying to pick up her pencils and know right away it was another joke.

She'd blame Michelle for sure.

"That does it," Michelle muttered. Now she was mad.

How could Jeff keep doing these things

to her? Why was he trying to get her in trouble?

Michelle began pulling at the pencils. She had to unstick them!

Mandy and Cassie came in. "What's the matter?" Cassie asked.

When Michelle explained, they tried to help. Cassie had scissors, which helped to pry up the pencils. Michelle pulled the last one loose with a snap just as Anna came in.

"You broke my pencil!" Anna said angrily.

Michelle looked down. It was true. The last of the four pencils had snapped in half.

"I'm sorry," Michelle said. "I was just trying to help. Someone glued them to your desk."

"Yeah, sure," Anna said.

"No, really!" Michelle insisted. She turned the broken pencil around in her fingers. She was searching for a sticky glue spot so she could show Anna she was telling the truth.

She couldn't find any sticky spots. The Joker must have used quick-drying glue.

Anna folded her arms. "I'm getting really sick of your dumb jokes. They aren't even funny," she told Michelle. "Why don't you just stop?"

"I told you, I . . ." Michelle let her voice trail off. How could she explain?

Anna turned away. Michelle went to her desk and sat down.

Jeff had struck again. Michelle was sure of it. Now her mind was made up.

Tomorrow she was going to get proof that he was the Joker. No matter what!

"Did you hear what he said?" Cassie asked.

"No, did you?" Michelle whispered.

It was lunchtime the next day. Michelle and Cassie were huddled together at a table in the lunchroom. Michelle held one of Lee's walkie-talkies in her hand. The other one was stuck under Mandy's shirt. Mandy was across the room, talking to Jeff.

RRRRRRRRUMBLE!

Michelle jumped. "What was that?" she asked.

"I think it was Mandy's stomach growling," Cassie told her. "Or maybe it was mine. I'm starving! Anyway, this isn't working. Mandy hasn't gotten Jeff to say anything about jokes. Come on, let's eat lunch."

"Wait!" Michelle begged. "I think I just heard Mandy say 'joke.' "

They bent over the walkie-talkie and listened closely.

"So—have you gotten any cool stuff from the joke store lately?" Mandy asked.

"All right!" Michelle cheered.

"No," Jeff replied. *"I haven't been there in weeks. Hey, I've got to go eat with Lee. See you later, Mandy."*

Michelle groaned. Across the room,

Mandy turned to them and gave a big shrug.

"Well, that's that," Cassie said. "Can we eat now?"

"I guess," Michelle said glumly.

She slumped at the table and put her head in her hands.

There had to be a way to prove Jeff was the Joker. There had to be.

But how?

Chapter
12

♥ That night Michelle could think about only one thing—proving Jeff was the Joker.

By morning she had an idea.

She would find a way to look into Jeff's backpack. If it was full of gag stuff, that should be enough proof.

As soon as she arrived at school, Michelle told Mandy and Cassie what she planned to do.

Cassie slapped Michelle a high-five. "Good idea!"

Michelle glanced at the pile of backpacks near the big double doors leading into the school. Jeff's pack had to be over there. All the kids left their stuff there while they hung out on the playground.

"Let's pretend we're getting something out of our own backpacks," Michelle suggested. "Then I'll sneak a quick peek into Jeff's."

"Okay," Mandy agreed. She sounded a little nervous.

With Cassie and Mandy right behind her, Michelle hurried over to the pile of backpacks.

"Which one is Jeff's?" Mandy asked.

Michelle stared at the mound of backpacks. There were at least twenty of them.

Cassie pointed to one. "I think it's that one. The blue-and-red one."

"Yeah, that's it," Michelle agreed. "He's had it since last year."

Michelle took a deep breath. She looked over her shoulder. No one seemed to be paying any attention to them.

She snatched Jeff's backpack out of the

pile. Then she knelt down. Mandy and Cassie stood in front of her so no one could see what she was doing.

Michelle hesitated. It felt wrong to go through someone else's stuff.

She had to find out if Jeff was the one playing those jokes, she told herself.

Michelle tugged the zipper open and peered into Jeff's backpack.

She gave a little gasp.

Jeff's backpack was filled with plastic spiders. And a tube of super-glue. An ice cube with a fly in it. A bag of balloons. A rubber pencil.

Everything anyone would need to play a bunch of tricks.

"I was right," Michelle said. "Jeff is the practical joker. Now, finally, I have all the proof I need!"

Michelle, Cassie, and Mandy grabbed their backpacks and moved away from the pile.

Michelle shot a quick look at Jeff. He

was playing catch. "I don't think he noticed a thing," she said.

"What do you think he's going to do with those balloons?" Mandy asked.

"I don't know," Michelle answered. "But I'm sure it will be something that gets me in trouble."

"So what are you going to do now that you finally have proof that Jeff is the Joker?" Cassie asked.

Michelle sighed. "I'm going to tell Jeff that I won't say anything to Mrs. Yoshida— as long as he stops playing tricks."

"That seems fair," Cassie agreed.

"I'll talk to Jeff at lunch," Michelle promised.

"Let's go in," Mandy said.

Michelle followed Cassie and Mandy into the classroom. She stuffed her backpack into one of the cubbies in the back of the room. Then she headed over to her desk.

She had to pass Jeff's desk on the way. Michelle swallowed hard. She wasn't looking forward to talking to him at lunch. She had no choice, though.

The bell rang, and Michelle rushed to her seat. Mrs. Yoshida liked them to take their places as soon as they heard the bell.

Michelle wanted to prove she knew the rules. She wanted Mrs. Yoshida to be proud of her. The way she used to be.

Mrs. Yoshida crossed the room to her big desk. She pulled out her chair—and frowned.

Uh-oh, Michelle thought. Something's wrong.

Mrs. Yoshida reached down and took something off her chair. She held it up so everyone in class could see it.

It was a big red balloon—filled with water. A note was taped to it. A note signed "The Joker" in big black letters.

"All right," Mrs. Yoshida said. "I want to know who put this water balloon here."

Michelle gulped.

Mrs. Yoshida was staring straight at her.

Chapter

13

♥ "We will not continue class until I find out who is responsible for this water balloon," Mrs. Yoshida said.

Michelle glanced around the room.

Anna was staring at her.

Erin was staring at her.

Lee was staring at her.

Amber, Denise, Evan, Lucas, Alvin, and Wendy were all staring at her.

Even Jeff was staring at her.

"We'll wait as long as it takes," Mrs. Yoshida said.

Isn't Jeff going to say anything? Michelle

thought. Is he *still* going to try to make me take the blame?

Mrs. Yoshida sighed. "Everyone put your head down, please."

Michelle crossed her arms and rested her head on them.

"Now I'd like the person who put that water balloon on my chair to raise his or her hand," Mrs. Yoshida said. "No one else in the class has to know."

"Everyone already knows Michelle did it," Erin muttered.

Michelle sat up. "I did not!" she protested.

"You did so," Anna called.

"No, I didn't!" Michelle couldn't stand it anymore. She jumped up. "I didn't put the water balloon on your chair, Mrs. Yoshida," she blurted out. "But I know who did."

Everyone in class sat up and stared at Michelle.

Michelle pulled in a deep breath. "Jeff

did it. He played all those other tricks too," she announced.

Mrs. Yoshida looked surprised. "Jeff, what do you have to say about this?"

"She's lying!" Jeff burst out. "Michelle is the one who has been playing jokes all week. Ask anyone."

Michelle glared at him. Then she turned back toward Mrs. Yoshida. "I did play some jokes Monday and Tuesday," she admitted. "But I promised I would stop after I squirted Wendy with the disappearing ink—and I did. Jeff is the one who did the other stuff. I can prove it."

Michelle rushed to the cubbies in the back of the room. She grabbed Jeff's blue-and-red backpack and marched up to Mrs. Yoshida.

Michelle unzipped the backpack and emptied it onto Mrs. Yoshida's desk. The fake spiders, the glue, the balloons, and everything else spilled out.

"Wow!" Erin cried.

Jeff jumped up. "That's not my backpack!" he exclaimed.

He ran to the cubbies and pulled out *another* red-and-blue backpack. "This one is mine," Jeff announced. He unzipped it and pulled out his favorite baseball cap. "See?"

Michelle stared at the backpack on Mrs. Yoshida's desk.

If it wasn't Jeff's, whose was it?

Mrs. Yoshida reached inside and pulled out a notebook.

Michelle's eyes widened. A name was written on the cover in large, neat letters.

Wendy Whipple!

Chapter 14

♥ "Wendy, you're the one who has been playing all those tricks?" Michelle exclaimed.

She couldn't believe it. Wendy was so quiet. She seemed so shy. How could she be the practical joker?

Wendy glared at Michelle. "You started it," she cried. "You squirted me with that ink!"

"I said I was sorry," Michelle answered. "I didn't know you would get upset. I just thought it was funny."

"Well, it wasn't funny," Wendy snapped. "It was mean."

"That's enough," Mrs. Yoshida said firmly. "I want to talk to both of you out in the hall. The rest of you, please begin reading chapter seven in your social studies books."

Wendy stomped out of the room.

Michelle followed her. She couldn't believe Wendy was still upset about the disappearing ink.

Mrs. Yoshida swung the door shut behind them. "Wendy, I have already spoken to Michelle about practical jokes. She promised me that she wouldn't play any more tricks at school. I want you to promise me the same thing."

Wendy stared down at her feet. "I promise," she muttered. "But Michelle—"

"I think Michelle knows she was wrong to play that joke on you. Isn't that right, Michelle?" Mrs. Yoshida asked.

"Yes," Michelle answered. "I saw you eating your lunch in the hall that day I squirted you, Wendy. I thought if I played a trick on you, you wouldn't feel so left out."

Wendy looked at Michelle. "Really?" she asked. "I thought you didn't like me. I thought you were being mean."

"I meant it when I said I was sorry," Michelle said.

"I'm sorry, too," Wendy said. She glanced at Mrs. Yoshida. "And I'm sorry I didn't tell you I was the one playing those jokes. I should have."

"Yes, you should have," Mrs. Yoshida agreed. "But I know starting at a new school can be hard." She smiled. "I think you deserve a second chance."

"And you also deserve to eat in the lunchroom, instead of in the hall," Michelle told Wendy. "Will you eat with me and Cassie and Mandy today?"

Wendy gave Michelle a big grin. "Okay!"

* * *

The next morning Michelle walked into class feeling happy. She was so relieved that the practical-joke mystery was solved.

She glanced across the room at Wendy and smiled. Wendy smiled back.

Settling into her seat, Michelle pulled her spelling workbook out of her backpack. Mrs. Yoshida usually started with spelling.

Mrs. Yoshida stood up. "Okay, everyone," she called. "This morning we're going to have a pop quiz on vocabulary. Please put your books in your desks."

Everyone groaned.

Michelle opened the top of her desk to put her workbook inside. Then she gasped.

A big fat spider stared up at her. A spider with red eyes and fangs.

After a moment, she realized it was only plastic. It sat right on top of a blueberry muffin.

Oh, no! Wendy doesn't know when to quit, Michelle thought.

Around the room, kids began to gasp as

they raised their desk lids. "Eeew! A spider!" Mary Beth wailed.

"Cool! A muffin!" Lee exclaimed.

Michelle's heart skipped a beat. Everyone in class has them! she thought. Muffins with spiders crawling all over them!

She jumped up. "I didn't do it," she cried. "It wasn't me, Mrs. Yoshida!"

"It wasn't me, either," Wendy declared. "Really!"

"It's all right," Mrs. Yoshida said. "This time I know who the Joker is."

"You know?" Michelle gasped. "Who? Who is it?"

Mrs. Yoshida smiled. "It's me!"

"You?" Michelle stared at her teacher. "But—but—"

"I decided we should have one last joke—a nice one," Mrs. Yoshida explained. "But this is the last trick I want to see in our classroom. And I mean that."

Mrs. Yoshida pulled out two cartons of juice and some paper cups from behind her desk. "We'll take a fifteen-minute muffin break," she told them. "Anyone who wants juice, come on up."

"Hey, thanks, Mrs. Yoshida," Erin said.

"Yeah, thanks," Evan called.

"Are we still having a pop quiz?" Anna asked.

Mrs. Yoshida laughed. "Not today," she replied.

Everyone cheered.

As she ate her muffin, Michelle glanced around the room. Everyone was smiling and laughing.

Except for one person.

Jeff.

There's something I have to do, Michelle realized.

She walked over to Jeff. "I need to talk to you," she said.

For a second she thought he wasn't going to answer. Then he glanced up at her. "What?" he asked.

"I'm sorry for telling Mrs. Yoshida that

you put the water balloon on her chair and played those other jokes," Michelle told him.

Jeff didn't say anything.

"And I'm sorry I snooped in your backpack—even though it turned out not to be *your* backpack," she added.

Jeff just shrugged.

Michelle took a deep breath. I better keep trying, she thought.

"Really, I am sorry," she said. "I shouldn't have done any of it."

Jeff hesitated for a second. "Okay," he said.

Michelle let out a huge sigh of relief. "Great!"

"There's just one thing," Jeff said.

Oh, no! Michelle thought.

"What?" she asked nervously.

"I just want to warn you." Jeff grinned. "Next April Fools' Day you better watch out!"

FULL HOUSE Stephanie™

Available from Minstrel® Books Published by Pocket Books

It doesn't matter if you live around the corner…
or around the world…
If you are a fan of Mary-Kate and Ashley Olsen,
you should be a member of

MARY-KATE + ASHLEY'S FUN CLUB™

Here's what you get:
Our Funzine™
An autographed color photo
Two black & white individual photos
A full size color poster
An official **Fun Club**™ membership card
A **Fun Club**™ school folder
Two special **Fun Club**™ surprises
A holiday card
Fun Club™ collectibles catalog
Plus a **Fun Club**™ box to keep everything in

To join Mary-Kate + Ashley's Fun Club™, fill out the form
below and send it along with

U.S. Residents – $17.00
Canadian Residents – $22 U.S. Funds
International Residents – $27 U.S. Funds

**MARY-KATE + ASHLEY'S FUN CLUB™
859 HOLLYWOOD WAY, SUITE 275
BURBANK, CA 91505**

NAME:_____

ADDRESS:_____

_CITY:_____ STATE:_____ ZIP:_____

PHONE:(____) _____ BIRTHDATE:_____

1242

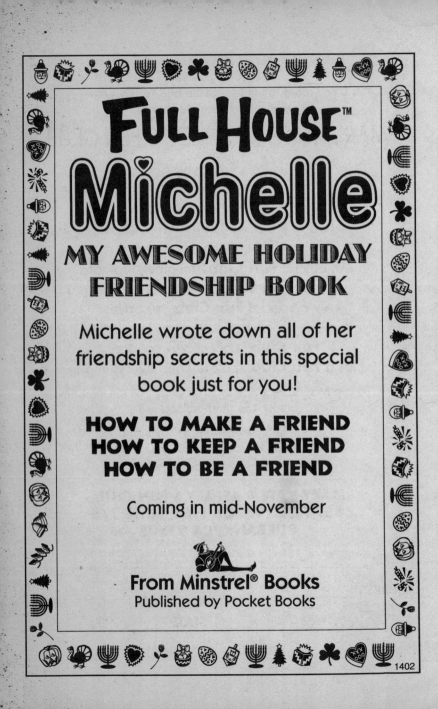

Full House™
Michelle

MY AWESOME HOLIDAY FRIENDSHIP BOOK

Michelle wrote down all of her friendship secrets in this special book just for you!

HOW TO MAKE A FRIEND
HOW TO KEEP A FRIEND
HOW TO BE A FRIEND

Coming in mid-November

From Minstrel® Books
Published by Pocket Books

1402